Con Mi Hermano
With My Brother

by/por Eileen Roe
illustrations by/ilustraciones por
Robert Casilla

Aladdin Paperbacks

A hardcover edition of *Con Mi Hermano* is available from
Simon & Schuster Books for Young Readers
The Library of Congress has cataloged the hardcover edition
as follows:
Roe, Eileen.
With my brother / by Eileen Roe ; illustrated by
Robert Casilla - Con mi hermano / por Eileen Roe ;
ilustraciones por Robert Casilla.
    p. cm.
Summary: A little boy admires his big brother and aspires
to be like him when he is older.
ISBN 0-02-777373-6
[1. Brothers—Fiction.   2. Spanish language materials—
Bilingual.]
I. Casilla, Robert. ill. II. Title. III. Title: Con mi hermano.
PZ7.R62Wi 1991 [E]—dc20 90-33983 CIP AC
0-689-71855-1 (Aladdin pbk.)

A universal Spanish that avoids regionalism is featured in
this book to make it most useful to all Spanish-speaking
children.

The publisher would like to thank Laurie Sale and Elena
Paz for their expert advice and careful readings of the
Spanish translation of *With My Brother*.

Aladdin Paperbacks
An imprint of Simon & Schuster Children's Publishing Division
1230 Avenue of the Americas
New York, NY 10020

First Aladdin Paperbacks edition 1994

Printed in Hong Kong by South China Printing Company
(1988) Ltd.
10 9 8 7 6 5 4 3
The text of this book is set in ITC Bookman Light.
Typography by Julie Quan and Christy Hale

A NOTE ON THE ART

The pictures in this book were done with watercolors on
illustration board. This nonabsorbent surface gives the
artist more flexibility with the medium, allowing him to
add and take away color. In several areas, pastels, colored
pencils, and acrylic paints were used to smooth and
highlight. The finished paintings were color separated and
printed using a four-color process.

For Samantha and her brother, Jason—E.R.

For my two models—
my son, little Robert,
and my nephew, Victor—R.C.

My brother is bigger and older than I.
He goes to school on the bus,

Mi hermano es más grande y mayor que yo.
El va a la escuela en el ómnibus escolar

and delivers newspapers in the afternoon,

y reparte los periódicos por la tarde

and plays ball at the park on Saturdays.

y juega a la pelota en el parque los sábados.

He doesn't always have time to play with me.

A veces no tiene tiempo de jugar conmigo.

But sometimes, I sit outside on the steps
and wait for him to come home.
When he sees me, he smiles and calls my name.

Pero a veces me siento en la escalera
y espero que llegue a casa.
Cuando me ve, sonríe y me saluda.

I run to him.
He grabs me
and we wrestle on the grass.
I always win.

Corro hacia él.
El me agarra
y luchamos en el pasto.
Yo siempre gano.

We walk down to the playground together,
my brother and I.

Caminamos juntos al patio de recreo
mi hermano y yo.

We play catch,

Jugamos a la pelota

and hang upside down
and talk together
until it's time to go home.

y nos colgamos boca abajo
y charlamos
hasta que es hora de volver a casa.

And sometimes in the evening,
when he finishes his homework,
we will do a puzzle together

Y a veces, por la tarde
cuando él termina sus tareas
trabajamos juntos en un rompecabezas

or I'll climb up on his lap
and we will read our favorite books

o me subo a sus rodillas
para leer nuestros libros favoritos

and sometimes he will say I'm getting too heavy,
that soon I'll be too big
to sit on his lap.

y a veces me dirá que ya peso tanto
que pronto estaré muy grande
para sentarme en sus rodillas.

But that's okay
because maybe then
I'll be big enough
to go to school on the bus,

Pero eso está bien
porque quizás para entonces
estaré bastante grande
par ir a la escuela en el ómnibus escolar

and deliver newspapers in the afternoon,

y repartir los periódicos por la tarde

and play ball at the park on Saturdays

y jugar a la pelota en el parque los sábados

with my brother.

con mi hermano.